AGENT RED (FATAL DEATH): TEAGAN STONE BOOK 6

TEAGAN STONE SERIES

AVA S. KING

LATEST RELEASES: AVA S. KING

Agent Red Fatal Memory Teagan Stone Book 1
Agent Red Fatal Target Teagan Stone Book 2
Agent Red Fatal Crime Teagan Stone Book 3
Agent Red Fatal Justice Teagan Stone Book 4
Agent Red Fatal Enemy Teagan Stone Book 5
Mirror of Lies -A Jessica Smith Book 1
Agent Red Fatal Death Teagan Stone Book 6
Mirror of Lust -A Jessica Smith Book 2
Upcoming Releases (2023/2024)
Chris Harris Mystery/Thriller Series
Agent Red Fatal: Revenge Teagan Stone Book 7
Agent Red Fatal: Pursuit Teagan Stone Book 8
Agent Red Fatal: Attack Teagan Stone Book 9
Agent Red Fatal: Mission Teagan Stone Book 10

I want to dedicate this book to my family and friends.
You are always with me, no matter where I go, and everything
you've taught me has made me a better person.

DISCLAIMER

This work of fiction contains strong language and explicit content and is only intended for mature readers. The story may contain unconventional situations, language, and sexual encounters that may offend some readers. This book is for mature readers (18+).

INTRODUCTION

Sign-up to Ava S. King's mailing list for news, new releases, and special offers.

www.authoravasking.com

SYNOPSIS

Teagan Stone has walked a fine line between life and death. This time, she's come across an enemy that doesn't care if she's the most trained killer or not. They only want one thing, and that's to see Agent Red brought to her knees. In a race against time, she will have to make the ultimate decision. Will she be able to save someone close to her or put the country she gave the oath to protect before her happiness?

CHAPTER 1

"Teagan, you need to stay calm. Breathe for me," Dr. Falk instructed, passing Teagan a cup of water and a napkin to wipe the tears pouring from her eyes. Everything was coming back up, and her demons that she tried to bury had shown up more and more.

"Now tell me, how are things going in your marriage?"

Teagan looked off toward the window in the office. Dr. Corinne Falk started working with Teagan a few months back to help her cope in the team. At first, she denied needing help, but her husband was adamant about having a better marriage. She needed to take care of herself and not let the The Firm become more important than her family. Teagan finally decided to commit to therapy because she wanted her kids to know their mother was healthy and present. Now at thirty-seven, the kids were older. She didn't want to miss any more time as they grew up before her eyes. Soon, they would be in high school, then college, and the house would be empty with just her and her husband.

"Fine." Teagan clenched the napkin in her hand.

Dr. Falk peered at Teagan, nodded, and wrote in her notepad. Teagan lifted the glass of water to her lips, then placed it back on the table.

"Where do you see yourself in five years, Teagan?"

Teagan shrugged her shoulders. Never in her mind did she think The Firm would bring her back in, let alone as the director, the person who puts lives at risk for national security.

"You don't know, or you refuse to answer?" Dr. Falk removed her glasses and held them in her hand.

Teagan sighed, closed her eyes, then opened them again, and balled up the napkin in her hand.

"I see myself still on the same cycle, rinse and repeat."

"Is that what you want?"

Teagan chortled.

"In this business, you don't get a choice to get out."

"I understand it's not a typical nine-to-five, but you have a choice."

Teagan wondered if the doctor knew how many people she'd killed because she was told it was best for the country.

"Dr. Falk—"

Ring!

Teagan glanced down at her cell phone ringing.

"You know I don't allow phones during the session," Dr. Falk chastised.

Dr. Falk discussed early on that Teagan was to be fully open during their sessions and to leave her phones off. Eventually, they compromised so she could keep it on vibrate, but Teagan forgot to switch it over when she walked in the office after picking up her kids from school.

"Sorry... Agent Red."

"We have a case," Spider said.

"What is it?" Teagan stood at the door with her back to the doctor.

"Teagan, we aren't finished," Dr. Falk called out. Teagan held her index finger up to pause her speaking.

"A kidnapping," Spider rushed out. Teagan reached in her pocket, grabbed her keys, and rushed out of the office. Dr. Falk jumped up, ran to the door, and called her name.

"Teagan! Mrs. Stone!" Dr. Falk yelled. Teagan ignored her demands.

"Who?" Teagan questioned and ran out of the office building.

"The last person we ever expected."

Teagan transferred the call to her Bluetooth, reversed out of the parking space, and turned into traffic as she drove back to the Agency.

"Get everyone to the office."

"I'm sending the details to your phone."

For a split second, she removed her eyes from the road and before she could make a turn… Boom!

The left driver's side was hit, swerved to the right side of the street, and barely missed the light pole.

"Pre…" Teagan mumbled as her eyes slowly drew closed as darkness surrounded her.

"Teagan! Teagan!" Spider shouted, as the blare of the horn sounded off. Someone ran a red light and careened to the side of her car. Sirens went off in the background. In a drowsy state, she tried to reach for her phone as blood slid down her cheek.

"Ma'am! Can you hear me?" a passerby called out, then reached his hand through the window to check her pulse.

"Mmmm…"

"Stay calm. Help is on the way," he reassured me.

A crowd formed around her car as witnesses watched

the other driver speak with the police, while the ambulance came to the side of Teagan's car and tried to free her.

* * *

HER EYES POPPED open at the brightness in the room. She glanced from the loud monitors beeping to voices surrounding her.

"Mmmmm..." Teagan slowly lifted her hand to her head and felt a bandage.

"She's awake." Christian went to her in the hospital bed and grabbed her hand.

"Christian..." she mumbled. He lifted the back of her palm to his mouth and pressed a kiss.

"Shush... you're in the hospital."

"What happened?" Teagan looked at Spider, the nurses, and the doctor in the room.

"You were in a car accident."

"Accident."

Teagan tried to sit up.

"Take it easy. Relax," Christian spoke.

"Mrs. Stone, you scared us for a minute." The nurse, Kathy, checked her pupils, then her pulse.

"Where are the kids?"

"Home. Don't worry. Can you tell us what happened?" Christian inquired.

"I got a..." Teagan's eyes rose in surprise at remembering a kidnapping.

The heart monitors went off, and she tried to climb out of the bed, Christian held her down.

"Teagan, calm down. You need to relax."

"No... the president... kidnapping." Her words jumbled together.

"Teagan, it's me Spider. Everything is under control."

Spider stood at the end of the bed and stared into her eyes.

"What about?" Teagan looked from the nurse to Spider. Christian knew the life they lived, but she'd already blurted out too much information.

"Everything is under control," Spider lied to keep her calm. He'd already had the team at the office gathering as much information as possible.

Finally, she stopped and relaxed back on the bed, while the nurse filled a cup with water and passed it toward her to drink.

"Thank you." Teagan took a gulp and closed her eyes momentarily to focus.

"I'll let the doctor know you're awake and get you some food brought up," the nurse said.

"Thank you," Teagan said, waiting for her to leave.

"You scared me." Christian cupped her chin.

"Did they catch who hit me?"

"A young kid," Christian replied.

"Are the kids really okay?"

"Yes, I told them you were working late." Christian pressed a kiss on her forehead. Teagan wrapped her arms around his shoulders.

That wasn't a lie because she often did work late and after so many years, it was natural that she'd miss family dinner. When Christian got the call, he was in the middle of work and had to leave the office to check on the kids and make sure they were okay with neighbors. Christian, at times, thought the worst call he'd get would be about Teagan out on a mission. Not a car accident in the city. He was thankful for Spider when he called.

"The doctor says you'll need rest for a few days, maybe a week."

"I have a new case."

Christian looked away.

"Teagan, you're no help to anyone at this time."

"This is something I have to work on."

"Listen to the doctor before you make any decisions. Promise me." Christian caressed her cheek.

The door swung open, and Doctor Nathaniel stepped over to her bed.

"Mrs. Stone, glad you're awake." Doctor Nathaniel listened to her heartbeat.

"When can I leave?" Teagan expressed.

He sighed and glanced from her husband to Teagan.

"I'd like for you to stay for the next forty-eight hours."

Teagan shook her head.

"Doctor, you don't understand."

He raised his hand up.

"Your team already informed me of your work, as much as they could."

"So you know that time is of the essence."

"There was no major internal damage, but you need to rest. If you can promise to take it easy, you can go."

"Of course, Doctor."

"Then in the morning, you're free to go."

Teagan started to speak.

"In the morning, Mrs. Stone. You might have a major position, but you're my patient at this moment."

"Thank you, Doctor." Christian shook his hand, then the doctor walked out of the room.

"Go home and be with the kids. I don't want them to worry."

"Are you sure?"

Teagan leaned up to kiss him on the cheek.

"Yes, I'll be home tomorrow. I don't want their routine interrupted."

"All right, don't give the nurses and doctors a hard

time." Christian stood and grabbed his jacket and keys off the couch.

"See you tomorrow."

Teagan picked up the remote and turned the television on with breaking news streamed across it. The chief of staff's sister is missing. Teagan's eyes rose in horror at the photos on the screen of the president's family in Italy. He's in America, while his mother and family traveled to Italy, after a trip to Paris. It was only a matter of time before Teagan would have to leave on the assignment to figure out what happened.

"At this moment, the president's family is secured," the reporter stated.

The door opened, and a nurse pushed through a cart of food. Teagan turned the TV off, sat up, and placed the remote on the bed.

"Enjoy." The nurse smiled, left the tray, and walked out of the room. Teagan lifted the lid off the plate to see only a note. Teagan's brows dipped low in confusion, as she picked the note up and flipped it open to a phone number. Teagan leaned over the bed, grabbed the phone, and placed it on her lap to dial the number.

"We've been waiting for your call."

"Who is this?"

"Glad to hear the accident didn't slow you down."

Her eyes rose in surprise.

"How do you know about that?"

"Get some rest, Agent Red. We'll be in contact soon."

The call ended, and Teagan slammed the phone down on the receiver, yanked the covers away, slid out of the bed, and tried to rush to the door when she felt pain on her side. The doctor had explained she'd be sore for a few days, maybe a week. Pushing through the pain, she opened the door and looked out at the empty nurses' station. She started to walk down the hall when the elevator opened, and the nurse that checked her vitals earlier approached.

"Mrs. Stone, you can't be out of bed."

"I need to find out who delivered my food."

"Is something wrong with it?" The nurse escorted her back to bed. Teagan scanned the empty hallway for any traces of the nurse who brought in the food.

"Do you know who else is working on this floor?" Teagan sat back down on the bed.

"Just me and Esther, but she's on break."

"What does Esther look like?"

"Tell me what this is about?" Her nurse saw the empty tray and removed it off the bed.

"Nothing, can I get some soup or something."

"What happened to the meal they brought up?" Nurse Kathy wondered.

"I… I… think it was for the wrong room." Teagan hesitated. Her head was still foggy from the car accident, then the phone call. She didn't know who to trust.

"Try to get some rest. I'll be back to check on you and bring you another meal."

Kathy patted her hand, picked up the tray, and walked out of the room.

CHAPTER 2

The doors of the conference room opened, and Teagan stepped inside in jeans and a black blazer, with her hair pulled back into a ponytail. Still the presence of a bandage across her forehead showed she was still in pain.

"I didn't think you'd be back so fast." Daughtrey jumped up out of the seat and came around the table to reach out for a hug. Teagan smiled and hugged Spider next.

"Should you be out so early?" Broderick inquired, and the room went silent.

"We have more important things to worry about. Besides, I'm fine."

Early this morning, Teagan was discharged from the hospital and went home while the kids were still asleep in bed. Christian helped her to shower and demanded she take it easy before she jumped back into work. Teagan was grateful for the outpouring of support from family and friends, but the bigger issue at hand needed to be fixed.

"If it becomes too much..." Spider said.

"I'll let you know." Teagan took a seat. Spider cleared his throat and pulled up the video footage from the day of the kidnapping. The room focused in on the screen as Spider slowed the video down. It showed a blurry shot of Jacqueline Anderson walking into the dressing room to try on a dress, then the clip jumped forward with a different timestamp.

"Where did you get the footage?" Daughtrey wondered.

"My connection at CIA," Spider mentioned and paused the video.

"What do we know? It's now been more than twenty-four hours." Teagan leaned forward and clasped her hands together.

"The president wants us to go in and extract her."

"From whom?"

"We don't know."

"I received a call last night."

All eyes turned toward Teagan.

"What did they say?"

"They knew about the car crash."

"You think it was set up?" Daughtrey remarked.

"Gregory, check the number on this burner phone. I'm not sure."

Teagan removed the phone from her pocket and placed it on the table.

"As of right now, we don't have jurisdiction and if we tried to go into another country…"

"Without any direct contact or information on who is behind this, we would bring political suicide to the president." Broderick sighed and ran a hand down his face.

Gregory typed on his computer, and Teagan noticed his brows dip in confusion.

"What do you have?"

"The number not only doesn't exist, but it's pinged globally from London to Los Angeles," Gregory answered.

"They're professional." Teagan stared off.

Ring!

The office landline rang.

Gregory leaned up and hit the answer button.

"Agent Red." The raspy voice from last night came through the phone.

"This is Agent Stone." Teagan leaned forward and motioned her hand for Gregory to trace the call.

"No need to trace this call. We'll give you the exact instructions," they stated.

"What do you want?"

"President Sanders has to answer to his crimes."

"Where is Jacqueline Anderson?"

"Not too fast, Agent." They laughed on the other end of the call.

"We don't negotiate with terrorists."

"Terrorists... I'd like to think of ourselves as saviors."

Gregory pulled up on the big screen a display of numbers that redirected across the globe. Teagan stood and walked around the table, staring at the projection screen.

"The president would only work through The Firm." Teagan pointed at the highest point where the numbers came from, with the majority directed from London.

"No matter for us. He needs to meet our demands."

"How's the weather?"

"Why?"

Gregory brought up the screen for a closer look at the area she pointed and noticed several restaurants and business.

"I'd hope your claim to have Noah's sister would be true, so I'd like to know how the weather is."

"Awww… Agent Red, are you trying to trace this call?"

"I already know you're in London."

The phone went silent.

"Before we move forward, I need to speak with Jacqueline."

"I'm sending over my demands. Once we've had confirmation, you can speak with Jacqueline Anderson." Unable to get the verbal confirmation that the chief of staff's sister was alive, Teagan blew out a frustrated breath.

"Nothing." Gregory slammed his hand on the top of the table.

"We have to give the president something," Spider commented.

"Gregory, get me everything you can on the call. Daughtrey, I want you to follow up with the hospital."

"What happened at the hospital?"

"Someone passed the phone to me, but it wasn't a real nurse."

"Someone pretended to be a nurse?" Spider blurted out.

"To get Noah's sister back home safely, we need to know if she's alive. All we have is a video of her entering a dressing room."

"Are we taking a trip?"

"Once you pinpoint the exact location."

"That's going to take hours, Teagan," Broderick said.

"Traveling to Italy or London will have to be done on a need-to-know basis."

Gregory listened to the voice recording from the call to break it down in parts, while Daughtrey rewatched the videos back-to-back. Broderick held the files on Jacqueline and Noah's family.

Three hours went by, and the team was still inside the conference room breaking down the call and videos. It was going on three in the afternoon, and Teagan needed to get home for the kids and rest. She'd promised Christian she wouldn't work too long and allow Spider to handle any major cases. She checked the time on her watch and sighed.

"Keep me updated on everything, Spider."

"Get some rest, Teagan," Daughtrey suggested, while she knew deep down the anxiety of everything was creeping up again. After the last case, she'd promised a trip as a family, and now it would be put on hold while the situation with Noah's sister was handled.

Spider walked out of the conference room with her and down to her office.

"Maybe you should rest. You still have the drama from the last senate hearing in your head."

Teagan patted him on the shoulder, eased her office door open, and sat at her desk. Spider leaned on the wall and watched her move with the temperament of a leader he knew she would become from the first time they met.

"What?" Teagan turned her computer on and logged into the classified files on the chief of staff and his family.

"I think we both know the answer to this question, so I won't ask again." He pushed off from the door and stepped toward her desk. Teagan looked up into his eyes.

"I'm staying." Teagan gathered up Jacqueline's background information, social media, and pictures at the White House.

"Do the guys know about your therapy sessions?"

Teagan lived with the memories of her time fighting many battles, then her transition back into the real world of being a wife and mom. The normalcy it brought was something she couldn't tear apart. Therapy helped, but telling her team about the regrets and nightmares would only put her in a vulnerable position.

"No, and I don't plan on telling them."

"You trust me?"

Teagan sat back in her chair, crossed her arms, and nodded at Spider.

"Trust the team, we've all been in your position."

An alert on the computer popped up with a new video stream. Teagan leaned forward and opened the attachment.

"If you want to see Jacqueline Anderson alive, you'll follow my directions." The video ended; Teagan replayed it again and turned the volume up. Spider angled around the desk to watch. They didn't recognize the voice, but Teagan figured it was the same person who called her in the hospital.

"I need a list of everyone who works at the hospital."

"We might not have that kind of time for that, Teagan."

"Then we make time. Right now, they're in charge. We need to make them sweat," Teagan declared. They both understood what she meant and would turn over every resource they have to bring her home safe from harm.

Ring!

"This is Teagan Stone," she answered.

"Hi, Mrs. Stone, this is Rachel from Tatum's school."

"Is she all right?" Teagan felt her heart sink with worry.

"She complained about an upset stomach, so she skipped lunch. I decided to let her go home early." Rachel's the assistant principal and understood Teagan's time from the Navy. People would think she'd always be absent from school functions, but nine times out of ten, she was there on parents' night to catch up with the daily activities of her kids.

"Thank you, Rachel. I'll be over to pick her up in a minute. Actually, I'll grab all the kids."

"I'll be here if you need anything." Rachel finished the call. Teagan reached across her desk to pick up her keys.

"Everything good with the kids?"

"Tatum's not feeling well. I don't want to worry Christian."

"Take care of the kids. I'll handle everything here."

Teagan slipped her purse on her shoulder.

"Thanks. Keep me updated, no matter how late."

"We got it from here, boss."

Teagan opened the door of her office, as Spider trailed behind. He pressed the elevator for the parking area.

"Is Sean taking you home?"

Teagan slipped her shades on.

"Yeah, Christian doesn't want me driving right now."

"I agree." Spider held the door open for her.

Teagan shook her head at how Spider treated her like she was the little sister and couldn't handle herself.

The doors closed.

* * *

TEAGAN HELD Tatum's head in her lap as the car drove out of the school parking lot with Sean driving. Once her eyes landed on Tatum, she knew her work would be limited.

"Mom, are you feeling better?" Cole glanced out the window toward his mother.

Teagan rubbed Tatum's back in circular motions.

"Why do you ask?"

"Dad said you were in an accident."

"Car accident, but I'm fine." Teagan caught Sean's stare through the rearview mirror.

"Good, I was worried."

Teagan reached over the seat and cupped his chin.

"Hey, you never have to worry about me."

"You're not invisible, Mom."

Those words made her pause in thought.

"I remember."

"Remember what, baby?"

"That time we were with those men."

Dr. Falk mentioned a few times that she thought the kids needed to speak with someone after everything they've experienced.

"Cole, you never have to worry about those men ever again."

Cole nodded in answer.

"Did you tell your mom about the ball tryouts, Cole?" Sean questioned from the front seat.

"What tryouts?"

"Not a big deal."

"Says who?"

"Mom..." Cole groaned.

The car arrived at their home.

"We'll talk about this later. Help your sister and grab her bag." Cole climbed out of the car. Sean shut the door, came around the passenger side, and picked up Tatum.

"Sean, she can walk."

"Let her sleep," Sean spoke, and Cole followed with CJ playing on his video game. Teagan slid the key in the door and dropped her keys and purse on the couch as Cole placed Tatum's bookbag on the floor.

"Do you have homework?" Teagan turned the TV on and lifted the headphones off CJ's ears.

"Yes, ma'am."

"Okay. Go change and get your homework done. I'll start on dinner." Teagan, kissed the top of his head.

"Do you guys need anything else?" Sean placed the comforter over Tatum.

"We'll be fine. Thanks, Sean."

"All right. Get some rest, boss. See you in the morning."

"Thanks, and Sean."

He paused at the door.

"I'm grateful for your friendship."

"Always, Agent Red." Sean winked and left her home. While she studied Tatum on the couch, she slid her coat off and laid it on the back of the couch. Teagan marched into the kitchen and opened the fridge to grab a bottle of water for medicine for Tatum. Right as she sat down on the couch, the door opened. Christian strolled in with mail in his hands.

"Hey, you're home early," Christian mentioned.

"Tatum didn't feel good." Teagan popped the water bottle open.

"Where are the boys?"

"Upstairs doing their homework."

"You okay?" Christian rubbed a hand up her arm and across her shoulder to lift her chin.

"Worried about a case."

"What else is new?"

"Can you sit with her, and I'll get dinner started."

"Sure, let me check in on the boys."

"Cole had ball tryouts."

Christian stopped at the end of the stairs.

"I forgot to tell you."

"Did you?"

Christian's brows dipped low in confusion.

"What are you saying?"

"Nothing."

"Did I not just rush to the hospital to make sure my wife didn't die!" Christian argued. Teagan peered up the stairs, hoping the boys didn't hear them.

"You're right. I'm sorry."

"Seems like you're always sorry," Christian fussed,

jogging up the stairs without waiting for a reply. Marriage still brought butterflies to her heart, but Teagan knew Christian wouldn't wait around for her to get out of her moods. If the case took over their lives, she needed to end the grudge soon and work in peace for everyone's sake.

CHAPTER 3

Spider shook his head as he replayed the video footage another time in the office. It had been more than forty-eight hours, and time was winding down. He'd eaten, slept, and washed at the office because he knew that was something Teagan would do.

"I think I got something." Gregory held a flash drive in his hand.

"Let it be something that helps."

"Wait! You can't go back there." The door pushed open with Secret Service agents and a woman very familiar to Spider and the team.

"Secretary Harris."

Secretary of Homeland Security Gloria Harris pulled no punches and met Teagan at every level when it came to The Firm. She believed in the program to an extent as long as they worked alongside her agenda. Whenever Teagan disagreed, things took a turn and put them at odds.

"Where's Director Stone?"

"Home," Spider answered.

"I'm right here, Secretary Harris." Teagan moved

around the security detail, strolled in the office, and stood next to Spider and Gregory.

"Glad you're feeling better after your car accident." Slight irritation in Gloria's voice made Teagan feel satisfied that no matter what anyone tried to do, they couldn't get rid of her stellar work that she'd proven to the president with The Firm. They hated her because she was cocky like them, but strategic in how she made her steps to get to where she was now. Never did she have to stoop down to the bitter level like Stanton or Harris to get to the top.

"Thank you, but why are you here?"

"Well, this case needs to be monitored because of the sensitive nature."

"Who authorized?"

"No one."

"I'll call you if we need you, but my team can handle everything."

"Are you sure? From what the news states, she's been gone for more than forty-eight hours," Gloria argued. Spider started to answer, but Teagan held her hand out to interrupt.

"You can't believe everything that's talked about in the media."

"Agent Stone, you're playing a dangerous game."

"Is there something we don't know?"

Gloria smirked and shifted from one foot to the next.

"No updates."

"Then I would like to get back to my case if you don't mind."

"It's your loss." Gloria stormed out of his office, with her men flanked behind her.

"What do you have, Gregory?"

"Are we going to talk about what just happened?" Gregory inquired.

"No, but I want to have someone keep an eye on her." Teagan placed her hand on her lower back.

"I had the same thought," Spider responded.

Gregory slid the flash drive in the computer and turned the volume up high.

All three listened with intense focus, leaning forward toward the computer.

The sounds were scattered noise and multiple voices until it was isolated to one sound.

"What is that?"

"Water, more or less."

"Are you saying they're near the ocean or something?" Spider mirrored Teagan's confusion.

"I don't know the exact location, but they're in Italy."

"How can you be sure?"

"Even though the tracking of the phone number pinged in multiple directions, it still showed in the same area that matches water."

Gregory clicked over to a satellite map and zoomed down to a red circle.

"Venice."

"Venice," Gregory and Spider answered at the same time.

"Get the pilot, and I'll call the president." Teagan reached in her pocket to pull out her phone. Gregory jumped up, grabbed his computer, and left the room. Spider extended his hand and dialed Daughtrey's office.

"Agent Stone," Noah answered the call. Teagan bit her bottom lip in hesitation on how much she should convey.

"Noah, is the president available?"

"Do you have news about my sister?"

"I think I should talk to the president first."

"Teagan, it's me. I know the business and how you deal

with family members in these situations. I can handle anything."

"If we have any major news, I'll keep you updated."

Noah sighed, and the phone went silent for a moment.

"Mr. President, it's Agent Stone."

"Teagan."

"Sir."

"Where are we with the case?"

"My team and I are heading to Venice."

"Italy?"

"Yes, sir."

"Does Noah know if this information?"

"No, sir."

"Better to keep it that way for now."

"I agree."

"We need this to end quickly, Teagan."

"I understand the predicament your country is in right now, sir."

"I'd hoped to avoid the international circus, but that ship has sailed."

"Secretary Harris was here, Mr. President."

"What do you mean?"

"Is there something I should be aware of concerning her or the Agency?"

"The Agency is not under my rule anymore. She shouldn't have a problem with anything that happens."

"By the way she stormed out of here, it may become a problem."

"All I want to know is when Jacqueline is on our soil."

"Any hands tied on this extraction?"

"You know I can't agree or deny anything that happens."

"Say no more, sir."

"Bring her home, Agent Red."

"Yes, Mr. President." They ended the call, and Teagan waited for Spider to finish. She paced in front of his desk and tapped her finger against her cheek.

He looked at her for a second as she mumbled under her breath.

"I know that look."

"Spider."

"You're not going, Teagan."

Teagan's head swung quickly toward Spider.

"Who's name is on the director's door?"

"As your friend, I think you should stay here after the accident. I mean you still look tired."

"I can handle myself."

Nothing would get solved at that moment, so Spider dropped the conversation. A knock came at the door.

"Come in," Spider called out.

"The van is ready," Daughtrey said.

"Let me call Christian, and I'll meet you downstairs."

"You got it, boss," Spider quipped sarcastically.

Teagan dialed his cell phone.

"Hello."

"Is Tatum feeling better?"

They decided to keep her out of school for another day, even when she was able to keep food down later that night. Teagan thought it was best to give her another day of rest.

"She's watching cartoons now." Christian chuckled. Teagan smiled at his words.

"I have to go out of town."

Silence.

"When?"

"Tonight."

He sighed.

"Not for long," Teagan hurried to say.

"You can't predict that, Teagan. Have you made another appointment with Dr. Falk?"

"Christian."

"If you're telling me you're going out of town, then I need to know when you come back, my wife will be the same woman I married. We just reconnected again after everything."

"You're right. I promise I'll give her a call."

"Where are you going anyway?"

"Venice."

"In Italy!"

Teagan squeezed her eyes shut. She'd said that flights out of the country wouldn't happen, and now she's going back on her word.

"I'll have protection."

"Seems you already made the decision."

"Kiss the kids for me."

"You're leaving right now?"

"Yes, but as soon as we land, I'll call you."

"I love you, Teagan."

"I love you more, Christian. Never doubt that."

* * *

THE NEXT DAY, Teagan finished a FaceTime call with her family back home as she sat in the rented apartment and drank her coffee. Gregory and Daughtrey went to the embassy in Rome, while Spider and Broderick checked over the weapons they'd brought with them.

"The car is ready." Sean stepped out on the balcony. Teagan had Gregory get a place not too far from the store that Jacqueline was last seen. The streets were busy with tourists around St. Mark's Square and the Grand Canal. It would have been a nice place to bring her family. Today, she was on a mission and needed to get in the right frame of mind to capture the last moments of Jacqueline in the store. As Spider directed Sean to the store, Teagan sat quietly in thought of how the next few days would go, searching over Venice. The president wanted an answer and demanded Jacqueline's return, but if anything happened that put them in danger, he'd deny they were ever in Italy on his orders. Possible arrest or death lay at her doorstep if something went wrong. No one sensed if she still suffered from her accident, and the weight of fighting or running around would be the bridge she'd have to cross in a moment's notice. Maybe she could have had Spider lead while she stayed home to recover mentally and physically. Emotionally, Christian could see the walls Teagan held up, but she was grateful he didn't fight her even more on flying out while Tatum was under the weather.

Sean parked the truck and slid the door open. Spider and Teagan followed, looking forward and backward, with patrons moving in and out of the store. One black van approached and parked behind them, filled with men she trusted from Interpol and local police.

"We'll stay out here." Semion, their contact from Interpol, leaned his head out of the car. Teagan nodded, and Sean held the door open. She glanced first up to the corners of the store for the security cameras. Spider removed a small device from his pocket to attach at the register for listening in on any conversations.

"Hello, I'm Arroya. Can I help you with anything?" the sales associate asked.

Teagan smiled and extended her hand.

"You have some lovely pieces here."

"Thank you. You're American." Arroya clasped her hands in front of her body.

"Yes, it's hard to get rid of the accent no matter where I go," Teagan joked.

"I love America. I hope to visit one day," Arroya said.

Teagan lifted a tag on a black dress.

"How long have you worked here, Arroya?"

"About two years. We get top-of-the-line clothing," Arroya explained grinning.

"You can keep a secret, right?" Teagan leaned in and whispered.

"Yes, of course."

Teagan glanced around the store. Spider headed around the register, placed the device, and slid to the back of the fitting room.

"I heard that someone powerful was kidnapped from here. I mean is it really safe to be here?" Teagan nervously shifted from left to right, blowing out a breath.

Arroya pushed a piece of her hair back and bit her fingernail nervously.

"Honestly, just between me and you, I was here that day."

Teagan's eyes rose in shock. She allowed Arroya the room to continue.

"What do you mean?"

"The American woman who was kidnapped. I saw her go into the back room."

"Wow, I'm surprised the police didn't keep you hidden."

Arroya shrugged her shoulders.

"I didn't see everything, just when she came into the store and went to the back."

"You're brave to even come back to work."

Teagan looked up when the door opened, and two more women came in laughing.

"Do you remember if anyone followed her that day?"

Teagan grabbed the black dress off the rack and held it up to her body.

"It was busy that day; I can't recall."

"Do you have this in cream?"

"Let me check our inventory."

"Thank you." Teagan walked alongside as Arroya scanned the tag into the computer.

She's either covering for someone or naive to the amount of trouble she could be involved with behind a kidnapping.

"Only comes up in black, gray, and red."

"The gray… I'd love to try that on."

Arroya stepped from behind the counter and went to the right side of the employee entrance. Teagan slid to the fitting room. Three of the doors were open, and the last one was closed. She glanced down at the shoes and tapped on the door.

"Spider."

He opened the door, and she slid into the room.

"Anything?"

"Check this out." Spider tapped lightly on the wall and pushed forward to a false mirror that led down a tunnel.

"Text Sean to head out front." Teagan stepped up on the stool and climbed through the tunnel, turning the light on her phone.

"Make sure—"

Spider closed the mirror back up as though it was never moved.

Underground, they could hear cars passing. If Jacqueline was brought from the tunnel to an awaiting car, it would be a perfect kidnapping.

"The cameras only end at the front entrance of the fitting room," he said.

Teagan scanned the walls and floors for any evidence.

"How did you get away from the sales girl?"

"She's looking for a dress."

Spider paused. Finally approaching stairs, Teagan slid her phone in her pocket and climbed up slowly, easing the door open to the street that angled a few blocks from a flea market and flower shop.

Spider stood next to her.

Teagan held her hand up to block out the sun.

Spider pointed to a camera at the flea market.

"Have Gregory get the footage."

"On it." Spider headed toward the market.

Teagan stared for a few minutes, then put herself in Jacqueline's shoes when they brought her out of the tunnel. It was a dead end near the shop, so they had to go in the direction of the market if it was a crowded day.

CHAPTER 4

Jacqueline sat on a chair with her face covered and her hands tied behind her back. She hadn't been able to sleep or relax since the day she was taken. Her life as a school teacher back in America was simple; she loved her life back home. This was supposed to be a fun trip with some of President Sander's family that Noah had arranged for her to attend. The one time she was away without security, her mouth and nose were covered with a cloth, and everything went dark. Once awakened, she was surrounded by silence, with people coming and going to bring her food. No one had attempted to hurt her physically.

"It's time to eat," a low raspy voice spoke.

Jacqueline sniffed the tears away.

"Remember, don't do anything crazy once I release you."

He untied her hands and placed the cold sandwich and a bottle of water in her hand.

Jacqueline quickly ate and drank, as he watched her movements.

"When we get paid, you can go."

Jacqueline wasn't naive to how the US dealt with terrorists.

"Can I talk to my family?"

He stood with both hands at his side.

"You had your one call."

"Please," Jacqueline mumbled.

"Doesn't work like that, princess." He slid a hand over her cheek. Jacqueline jerked back.

"They won't pay you."

"If they want you alive, they will." He snatched the bottle of water out of her hand, tied her back up, and locked the door. All she could do was pray her family could find her remains if something happened.

* * *

HIS PARTNER SAT on the couch with his feet up, typing on his computer with the TV playing.

"Did she eat?" Godfrey asked; he was the computer whiz who made the call to Teagan. Both men, in their late twenties, went against the normal society standards and worked against government entities. The idea to grab Jacqueline wasn't done lightly, and they took the job because the money sounded good enough for them to take and run.

"Yeah."

"You didn't touch her, did you, Alex?"

He smirked.

"She's not to be touched."

"Says who?"

Heels clicked against the floor and stopped at the edge of the door.

"Me." She held shades against her bottom lip.

Both men sat up straight.

"I didn't touch her." Alex rolled his sleeves up, showcasing his tattoos.

"Has she eaten?" she asked.

"I gave her a sandwich and water like you said."

"My men will have the money wired to you."

"You never told us why you wanted her kidnapped." Godfrey stared at her.

"You never asked."

She took a seat on the edge of the couch.

"I didn't find anything about you, no birth certificate, or anythimg. It's like you never existed." Godfrey looked at her in confusion.

She smiled.

"Godfrey, my dear boy, you aren't the only one good at computers."

"Then what's your real name because Blair De Leon is fake." Godfrey's voice was a little shaky.

She stood, removed her jacket, and passed her shades to her guard.

"Oskala Kingston." She reached behind her back, pulled out her gun, angled it toward Godfrey, and shot him between the eyes.

"Please don't!" Alex shouted, and Oskala held her finger up to her lips and motioned for him to be quiet.

"I promise you won't feel a thing." Oskala pulled the trigger.

"Where are we taking them?" one guard questioned.

Oskala looked at him, and he passed her a cigarette. Holding up the lighter, she took a pull.

"Burn them and grab her from the back."

Oskala Kingston waited years for her moment to get

revenge. Teagan Stone would know the pain of death before she flew out of the country. Jacqueline was a pawn in a bigger game that Oskala didn't care if she became another victim after the way they'd hindered her family's life when they took Diablo from her.

CHAPTER 5

Secretary Gloria Harris held a conference at the state department on the updates on Jacqueline's disappearance. Her way of inserting herself in the case would be through back channels since the president didn't explain why Teagan and most of her team flew out in the middle of the night.

"Hello, I'd like to take this moment to say a few words. For our country, I know we all are praying for Jacqueline's safe return."

The flashes of the camera continued.

Gloria cleared her throat.

"Briefly, I want to let you know that President Sanders and this administration are doing everything possible to bring Jacqueline home safely."

"Secretary Harris, who is running point on her rescue?"

Gloria smirked on the inside and held a steady gaze. Preston, a reporter for The Daily Beat, was her inside man when she needed to look favorable in the public's eye.

"Classified, but I can say we have our best people working the case."

"You say the best, but no word if she's alive or dead," Preston followed up.

"When it comes to international friends, we have to be diligent to not give out the wrong information."

"Can you tell us if a ransom has been spoken of at all around the White House?"

"Again, Preston, classified."

"My source said Teagan Stone of The Firm has left the country."

Gloria wanted to give him a high five in that moment because it riled up the other reporters, and more hands raised.

"Not sure where you got your information. Agent Stone handles many cases."

"So, you don't deny her involvement."

While he put more focus on Teagan, it showed the credibility lacking in President Sanders' judgment to have them deal with a matter after all of the bad blood over the years.

"Don't put words in my mouth, Preston. The Firm is a trusted agency."

Teagan switched the channel and dialed the president's number.

"She's setting us up," Daughtrey hissed, watching the foot traffic outside the building.

Gregory sat in the love seat, condensing all the market footage surrounding that day.

"What do you think her endgame is?" Broderick stepped in the room.

"Same as everyone else. Appearances."

"She's using the kidnapping to her advantage." Spider held out bags of food and passed them around.

"Teagan, I need an update," Noah answered the phone in a rush.

"Is he there?"

"Be honest with me," Noah muttered.

"We don't have her, but I feel she's still alive."

He sighed.

"I guess no update is a good thing."

"Not if they saw the conference from Secretary Harris."

"The president is calling a meeting now," Noah remarked.

"I'm sorry, Noah. She's using Jacqueline to get ahead."

"It's Washington; I don't expect anything less."

"We went to the store and saw how they took her out."

"Tell me."

"It was a false wall in the room."

"Oh my God."

"I can explain more later, but I need to handle something first. Let the president know we will be in touch soon." Teagan rose off the couch with the food Spider brought and walked to the back of the apartment. Sean stood at the door.

"Is she awake?"

"She stopped screaming about two hours ago." Sean opened the bedroom door for Teagan. To find answers, she would need to get even dirtier. She brought Arroya back to the apartment and watched her sleep. Teagan would have preferred to avoid torture as much as possible. However, the only way to get Jacqueline back would be to go back into the dark place she had blocked out. There was a television with only one channel that showed repeats of a cartoon, a chair, and a blacked out window in the room. It brought to mind her time in captivity.

Arroya moaned, as her eyes fluttered open.

"Are you hungry?" Teagan held up the chicken pasta.

"Who are you?"

"I told you."

"You're an American, but I can see now you're more than a customer here to buy a dress," Arroya said in her thick Italian accent.

"Are you hungry? I brought you some food."

"I want to go home."

Teagan smiled and placed the food on the bed.

"Where is she?"

"Where is who?"

Teagan chortled and scratched her cheek.

"You aren't stupid, Arroya. I know you know why you're here."

Arroya looked at the door and back at Teagan.

"It's scary, I know, but remember, I can help you."

"I don't know anything."

"You know why I'm here."

Arroya shook her head.

"I do things that the government can't do."

"Why are you telling me this?"

"Because if you don't tell me what I want to know, I'm afraid you're never going to see your mother or grandmother again."

Teagan stood from the bed and picked up the food.

"Now are you hungry?"

Arroya hesitated for a few minutes, then reached out to grab the bag.

"I was given a note and a phone one day."

"What time?"

"When I walked out of my apartment. It was on the ground."

"No one saw it being placed."

"No."

"What about your mother or grandmother?"

"I didn't say anything to them. I just made a phone call."

"What did the note say?"

"It just held a phone number so I dialed." Arroya cut into the pasta.

"Why didn't you go to the police?"

"I thought it was a joke at first. Then, when I checked my account, I had money deposited."

"What did they say over the phone? How did they sound?"

"Basically, they asked me to keep this woman occupied and show her dresses, so I did."

"So, pile her up with clothes, then she'll be in the shop long enough for them to make a move."

Arroya wiped a tear across her cheek.

"Am I going to jail?"

"How much did they pay you?"

"A million."

After a knock, the door opened, and Sean peered in and motioned for Teagan.

"Are you going to kill me?"

"Finish your food." Teagan stepped in the hallway.

Sean closed the door.

"They found two bodies that washed up," Sean said.

"Shit." Teagan pinched her nose.

"We don't know if it's a woman or not."

"Keep a watch on her."

"You know we can't let her walk away," Sean commented.

To her dismay, she knew he was correct. That comes with being caught up in the world of danger and the work they did in The Firm. It was getting late, and she needed to get an ID on the bodies before the media got wind of anything.

"We'll handle it when we get back." Teagan stalked back into the living room and grabbed her jacket, cell, keys, and gun.

"A contact has the bodies ready for us to view." Spider explained.

"Is it a woman?"

"No, two men."

"Then why do we have to view?"

"My contact said they were found with interesting writing on their bodies."

* * *

"*Jacqueline*," Daughtrey read the words on Godfrey's torso.

"Do we have a time of death?"

"Yesterday around the afternoon," the coroner explained.

"Damn it, someone's playing with us."

"Where exactly?"

Coroner lifted the file and read off the details.

"Both men were shot and thrown in the water, no witnesses. But we picked them up near Calle del Pestrin."

"Thanks."

"We can get some guys to stake out the area." Daughtrey removed his phone and dialed Broderick.

"Be discreet until we get there," Teagan mentioned.

"Are you American detectives?"

"Something like that. But did you find any ID or phone on them?"

"Nothing besides their clothes."

"What are you thinking?" Daughtrey questioned.

Teagan rubbed her chin.

"If they're dead, that means someone bigger is in control."

"And I need to get Jacqueline out before they kill her."

"Whoever's in charge doesn't care about the money."

Daughtrey and Teagan climbed in the van, and Sean shut the door.

"We're dealing with someone smart, who's not afraid of any political ramifications."

Thoughts ran in her mind, as she looked out the window at the apartment buildings, curious if someone was watching when they arrived and left.

"The story Arroya told, do you think it adds up?" Daughtrey wondered.

"Can you stop at the market, Sean? I want to grab a few things."

"Gotcha, boss." He knew Teagan was getting frustrated and ready to head back home. If they didn't find Jacqueline soon, it would be seen as failure, and that's something she couldn't live with.

Ten minutes later, Sean arrived at the market near where the bodies were pulled out of the water. Sean climbed out of the car and opened the back door for her to step out. Teagan peered at the sign, then over to the kids playing outside on a bike. Daughtrey came around the passenger side door and started to walk alongside Teagan when a car careened around the corner, blasting toward the market.

"Get down!" Daughtrey yelled, as he reached for his gun to cover Teagan. Sean managed to block Teagan's view, as the bullets went through his chest, leg, and neck.

"Sean!" Teagan screamed. The kids cried and dropped to the ground. The black-tinted Mercedes Benz drove down the street and made a sharp turn while people scrambled for safety.

"Teagan! Teagan!" Daughtrey shouted, as he jumped up from behind the car and ran to Sean and Teagan. Sean's lifeless body lay on top of her with his eyes closed. She continued to call his name as tears fell down her cheek.

"Sean, please, wake up."

Daughtrey shifted Sean's body to the side, checked his pulse, and removed his phone from his pocket.

"Call the ambulance!" Teagan screamed at the store workers. Everyone watched as the two tried to revive him.

"Are you hit?" Daughtrey grasped her arm, and she pushed him away.

"Don't touch me!" she screamed.

A few moments later, Spider and Gregory arrived, along with the police and ambulance.

"Teagan, we need to check you out," Daughtrey said.

Her hands shook, and her eyes peered around the crowd, unable to comprehend what they were saying.

"It's Spider. Hey, focus on my voice," Spider calmly stated, wrapped his jacket around her arms, and helped to lift her from the ground.

"We need to get her back to the apartment. Too many eyes out here," Daughtrey remarked. Sean's body was loaded on the stretcher.

"Where are they taking him?" Teagan demanded, walking over to the police and the ambulance to speak from the corner.

"Teagan, he's gone," Spider softly said.

"Spider, shut up! He's not gone."

All eyes looked at her. Teagan clenched and unclenched her hands, blowing out a long-held breath.

"I need Agent Red at this moment," Spider whispered in her ear.

Teagan stopped her pacing.

Daughtrey and Gregory jumped in the car and waited.

"I want his body shipped back immediately. Notify the president, and everything should be paid for by me."

"I understand."

"No one touches him without our people watching.

Make sure the family is told before the media gets the information."

"Anything else?" Spider held the door open to the backseat for Teagan to slide inside.

"Gregory."

"Pulling footage and plates," Gregory answered.

"I'm going to stay with Sean's body," Daughtrey said before she could ask.

"Kill Arroya." Teagan leaned her head back on the seat and closed her eyes.

Sean had been more than a driver and friend. He'd become like a brother to her and an uncle to her kids, and Christian became close with him, even taking him on golfing trips often. On holidays, he'd bring the kids presents, and Sean would pop up at birthday parties and spoil them more than the grandparents. He kept her abreast of the kids' after-school activities and drove them around when she wasn't available. It would be hard to explain how he would no longer be around. How would they move on as a family and team? He was a longtime military man and brother who joined the Agency and didn't mind working for a woman when it wasn't popular. Teagan knew when she retired, Sean would do the same, and they joked often that no one else could put up with her high demands and annoying attitude. Spider reached over and grabbed her hand.

"He did what he had to do."

"That's what he told me often." Teagan reflected on her conversations with Sean during long drives to work.

CHAPTER 6

skala's Past.

Diablo laughed with his men in the backyard of the mansion he and his wife, Oskala, recently purchased. He could hide his lovers from his wife, while she lived in Colombia, but she'd fought with him to live together as one. Even though he held business as the Don of Kingston Cartel, no one knew of Oskala, and he'd planned to keep it that way, especially from the woman he'd met at the art show. The American beauty captured his attention, and he wanted to continue the pursuit without interruption from Oskala.

"Gentlemen, I want you to meet my beautiful wife Oskala." Diablo and Oskala went back from their youth. Their families wanted them to marry, and she'd been trained to become his wife one day. She knew all about his business as a drug lord and helped him many times when someone needed to be taken care of. What Diablo didn't know was that Oskala was deadlier than his top killers. A trained sharpshooter, with a fetish for knives, she could seduce a man within one minute and then slit his throat.

42

The reason she was back in their home country was because Diablo thought Oskala would continue to be alone as the doting wife. They didn't have any children, and she'd never wanted to damage her body. The only things that motivated her were money, power, and her husband. Oskala lifted her hand toward the guests and smiled.

"Gentlemen, I hope my husband isn't boring you." Oskala grinned and placed her hand on his chest.

Diablo laid his hand on her lower back.

"Who did Diablo have to kill to marry you?" one of his business partners questioned.

"My husband isn't the only one who's lucky."

"Don't be fooled by that smile. She could be deadly." Diablo squeezed her waist.

"He's modest. I can be deadly but sweet at the same time." She winked at them and pulled out a cigar, and all the men clamored to light it for her.

"Thank you." She blew out the smoke and turned to walk toward the pool in only her bikini top and thong with high heels.

"Gentlemen, as you can see, I have bigger things to handle. I'd like to conclude our business."

"What you're asking is not easy, Diablo."

Diablo took a sip of his cognac.

"I want what I want."

"To get into America, you need resources and a plan."

"My money is good."

"Not about money."

Diablo waved him off.

"Either you get the trucks through Mexico or not."

"The governor won't let that happen."

Diablo smirked and stared at his wife.

"I might have another idea."

* * *

"Gloria, I understand your concerns, but my hands are tied," the governor of Mexico, Fernando Perez, spoke into the phone. The door of his home creaked open as heels clicked against the wooden floors.

"You're getting a cut, Governor Perez. Don't pretend you care about your people."

He grunted, turned around in the chair, and faced the wall of pictures.

"I run everything that goes in and out of Mexico. As of now, I plan on keeping it local." He tapped his finger on the side of his forehead.

"I'm hearing whispers of the Kingston Cartel creeping on your territory."

The governor went silent.

The door knob turned quietly, and Oskala, in a maid's uniform, held a tray with a drink, and a knife underneath.

"The Kingston Cartel can't touch me. Do you understand?" He leaned up out of the chair and cursed. Oskala laid the tray down on the desk, smiled, and stepped around to face him. His eyes ballooned wide.

"Who are you?"

"Diablo sends his regards." Oskala drew the knife across his throat and picked up the phone.

"Governor! Governor!"

"The governor is unable to take your call."

"I know this is Diablo's doing."

"If you know, then you should be scared."

"He won't get away with this."

"We'll meet, Gloria, soon." Oskala giggled.

"Who are you?"

"Someone who doesn't like it when Diablo is disrespected."

"Is the governor really dead?"

Oskala stared at his dead body.

"You can make a guess." Oskala ended the call and walked out of the room.

* * *

A FEW DAYS LATER, Diablo sat at the table reading the paper when his butler escorted some business associates into the dining room.

"What have you done, Diablo?" He was held back by the arm of another business associate.

Diablo sat back, smiled, and peered at Oskala.

"Oscar, take a seat. Are you hungry?"

"You killed him!" Oscar shouted, throwing his hand in the air.

Diablo poured orange juice in his glass.

"Killed who?" Diablo took a sip and cut into his steak and potatoes.

"Governor Perez is dead, essentially guaranteeing your position for Mexican trucking."

"Oscar, are you scared?" Oskala spoke up, grabbed the knife, and pointed it toward him.

"The men are talking," Oscar fussed.

Oskala laughed, cut her apple in two, and took a bite.

"Sorry to hear about the governor's death. Hopefully, he didn't suffer," Diablo said.

"I know you're behind this, Diablo. Just remember it can come back to bite you."

"Is that a threat?" Oskala inquired.

"Keep Oskala on a leash, Diablo." Oscar shifted and walked out.

"She's dangerous, Diablo."

"I like them dangerous," Diablo replied and watched Oskala stand, saunter around to his chair, and sit in his lap.

"Remember, I'll always have your back, Diablo," Oskala said.

"I know."

Oskala stayed in the background as Diablo worked his connections and ran the Kingston Cartel. Years later, a raid happened at his compound, and Oskala moved back to her home and focused on the woman he was seen with in photos at certain events. She knew he wasn't completely faithful, but how could he allow himself to be taken down so easily. Now, she had to rebuild the life they had together. Oskala focused the dots on everyone that Diablo encountered, and she plotted to bring them all down, starting from the top with the woman he cheated on her with. Once she learned the ins and outs of The Firm's workflow and the US government's handling of Diablo's arrest, Oskala had a plan in motion and would let them all see how the Kingston Cartel would always be around.

CHAPTER 7

*P*resent.

"She's sleeping." Oskala put the fork down from eating her salad and picked up her phone.

"The shooting wasn't shown on the news." Oskala's guard stood against the chair of the kitchen table. Oskala sipped on her coffee.

"We have to make a bigger move."

"What else can we do?"

"I have something lined up. Just watch and see." Oskala dialed a number.

"Action Nine News, this is Kailey."

"Hello, Kailey, I don't want my name to be used, but I have information about the Jacqueline Anderson kidnapping."

"Can I have your name?"

"No names please, or I'll call someone else with this information."

"I understand. What information do you have?"

"Two people were found dead, connected to the kidnapping of Jacqueline."

"Who are the two people?"

"All I know is that it's two men. Check with the Italian police." Oskala hurriedly hung the phone and grabbed her coffee.

"Are we moving her?"

"No. After the news gets out, she's going to come for us." Oskala picked up her gun next to her purse and held it up.

"All of our people are ready to move when you're ready."

"Keep them on standby. I have a few things to wrap up." Oskala rose, lifting her purse, gun, and shades.

"Do you need me to come with you?"

"No, I won't be long."

* * *

OSKALA SAT on a boat with her contact from America.

"I can't be seen with you."

"You worry too much, my friend."

"Why did you kill them?"

"They served their purpose."

Oskala sipped on her champagne.

"I can't give you any more information."

"Are you sure?" Oskala laid her hand on his chest.

"It's over, Oskala. You've made your point."

"My point is just getting started." The boat pulled back up to dock, and Oskala stood and climbed out of the boat.

"Oskala! I can't help you if you step over this line."

"Broderick, the line has been crossed when you fucked Diablo over."

Oskala switched over to the limo waiting for her to slide in. The door shut, and the limo drove off. Her plan to infiltrate Teagan's men wasn't easy, but the secrets Brod-

48

erick held fell into her lap. Diablo told her to use those tactics of a beautiful face to make men do anything she wanted, and Broderick was an easy mark. His gambling debts came back to haunt him, and the people he owed were back to collect. Oskala owned those debts. A few minutes later, they arrived at the warehouse. Oskala stood around a table of her men who were loyal to Diablo. To see a familiar face from Oscar was interesting because of how he hated her back in the past.

"Oscar, thank you for joining us."

"You made the choice easy when I looked at my bank account," Oscar responded.

"Men and their money."

"What plans do you have, Oskala?"

"The ultimate plan is to bring the Kingston Cartel back to the top."

All she heard were gasps.

"Who is in charge?"

"The only person Diablo trusted with his empire... me." Oskala removed her jacket and laid it on the back of the chair.

"No woman should lead the cartel." Oscar leaned up against the table.

"Oscar, times have changed. You have to wake up to what is right in front of you."

Oskala angled around the table to stand behind Oscar.

"You're being a fool."

Oskala planted her hands on his shoulder.

"What I'm doing is taking the business to another level you fools could never have imagined."

"Diablo wouldn't want you in charge."

"Diablo put his entire life in my hands and taught me everything. I can lead."

"So why are we here then?" another mafia boss stated.

"I need your resources to bring Kingston back to where we want to be."

"What percentage are you negotiating?" Oscar wondered.

"Give us access to your men, and you'll receive five percent of the first kilo."

"Twenty," Oscar blurted, and Oskala narrowed her eyes.

"Oscar, you're in a position to bring in a lot of money from this deal."

"If we give up so much, and you end up taking the cartel to a bigger level, that's more eyes from the police. We deserve compensation." He pointed in the air.

"Ten percent and let me say, you don't want me as an enemy," Oskala announced.

Everyone went silent.

Oskala picked up her jacket.

"You know what I am capable of, gentlemen. Don't disappoint me."

CHAPTER 8

President Sanders sat in the Oval Office and listened to his staff break down the situation with Jacqueline in Italy. The Kingston Cartel was behind the kidnapping, they'd discovered. His last campaign almost ended when Diablo's name was brought back into the media. There was a point when the media posted outside Noah's family home and searched through his family background to associate them with an international crime ring.

"Do we have exact eyes on her?" President Sanders leaned back in his chair. Noah stood stoic near the side door that led to his office.

"Nothing yet," the deputy chief of staff said.

"How did we miss this! I want a full investigation." President Sanders glowered at his team of military staff and FBI.

"Diablo was watched at all times; there is no evidence of outside communication." FBI coordinator Ryan Magnum showed him the photos of Diablo under custody at the time after the first run in with Teagan.

"We continue to be behind these incidents, and it makes me wonder if we have a leak in the White House." President Sanders glanced around at his team. Everything of that day played across the media from news stations to internet posts about the abduction. President Sanders's administration had more to accomplish before his term ended. He felt if he couldn't keep safe the people who worked closest to him, it would show in the public opinion he wasn't living up to the position of being the president of the United States. The confidence he displayed often in front of the camera was slowly fading away as the days went on without a word from the team.

"Which means we need to think of alternatives."

"Secretary Harris." Secretary of Homeland Security Gloria Harris extended a hand to the president, removed her coat, and placed it on the back of the couch.

"Mr. President, I looked from all angles."

"Are you saying to put my sister in harm's way?" Noah called out. Gloria looked over her shoulder at Noah and slid one hand in her pocket.

"Hopefully, I'm not speaking out of turn. But as the chief of staff, you're too close to the recovery mission."

"That's my sister," Noah scoffed, pointing at his chest.

"Noah," President Sanders spoke and glanced at him. Gloria cleared her throat.

"I know you have your team out there, but we need a heavy presence to show that we don't take the kidnapping of the chief of staff's family lightly." Gloria motioned her hand at Noah.

"What are you proposing?"

"Military intervention."

President Sanders shook his head, stood, and turned to the window in his office.

"I can't do that."

"Either we make a statement now, or we lose our power." Gloria crossed her arms over her chest.

Noah understood the president's hesitation, even though he wouldn't want to put the world at war. But to know he didn't try everything to bring her home caused a sharp pain in his chest.

"We wait until we hear from Teagan. I trust her decision."

"That would be a major mistake, Mr. President."

"I hear you, Gloria, but we need to give them more time."

"The people who have her don't care about some agent you've depended on in the past. We need to fight with fire." Gloria raised her voice.

"Give me the room." The president waved for them to leave. Gloria turned to leave the room, and he stopped her.

"You stay."

Noah stared at Gloria, then walked to his office.

The president closed his eyes in thought.

"If there's something you know, I suggest you tell me."

"Excuse me, Mr. President."

"What do you know about Jacqueline's kidnapping?"

"Nothing."

"If we hear you're behind anything…"

"Sir, I'm loyal to our country and to this administration," Gloria said.

"Teagan is in charge of Jacqueline's case. Either you work with her, or you're against us."

"Sure thing, Mr. President." Gloria slid her hands in her pockets and left. Noah came back into the room and stood next to the president's desk.

"She knows something."

"About Jacqueline?" Noah pressed.

"We've had too many people screw us behind our backs. Keep an eye on her."

"The call never came, and so we were waiting on confirmation from Teagan."

"Give them time. She's on to something."

"After Sean's death, we don't know how this will play out for us."

"Have the arrangements been made for his funeral?"

"In the planning stages now."

"Make sure you have a note and flowers sent from me."

"Are you going to give a speech on the incident with Sean?"

"Taylor gave a briefing earlier on and sent our condolences."

"We're going to get Jacqueline back, Noah."

"I know."

"If you need to take some time, I understand."

"Until she's back on our home soil, I won't be able to rest at home."

Knock! Knock!

"They're ready for you, sir." Taylor poked her head in the office. The president buttoned his suit and walked out of the office to the press briefing room.

* * *

"Please have a seat," the president spoke to reporters.

"The president will take a few questions, but he won't be able to stay long," the press secretary stated.

"Mr. President, do we know who's behind what has happened in Italy?" The reporter held his hand up.

"At this time, we can't release that information."

"Some people say this is about your connections to The Firm."

"Paul, I won't get into any rumors."

Another reporter raised their hand.

"What is the latest status of Jacqueline's release?"

"Mary, we're doing everything to work with our partners to make sure Jacqueline is home safe."

"With all due respect, Mr. President, you've already lost a man. How can the American people trust you to bring Jacqueline home safely?"

The president shifted from one side to the next, clearing his throat.

"Mary, what I would say to you and the American people is that we have the best military in the world and agents we trust to do their jobs. We've lost a great man, but he would want us to continue and bringing her home."

"The president has another call. We'll have him come back." Taylor ended the press briefing, and all of the press threw out questions as he left.

Teagan closed the door to her car and stared at the camera pointed at the shop Jacqueline frequented the day she was taken. As the time ticked, she knew it was now or never to make a move and bring her home safely. After the president spoke, and outlets received a tip that two bodies were found connected to her disappearance, Teagan figured they'd escalated. She checked her holster and vest and walked to the back of the building. Daughtrey came up behind her with a tool kit in his hand. After the night of the ambush, Gregory was able to get more intel that was shocking and surprising about Diablo.

"Watch out."

Teagan looked behind her as the people went about their business and didn't notice or say anything about two people lurking around an apartment building.

"Got it." Daughtrey unlocked the back door of the building, and Teagan followed him.

"Stay behind me," Teagan said.

"What made you pick this place?"

"I got a feeling."

A cat ran through the hallway.

"Shit!" Daughtrey cursed.

Teagan noticed an older couple coming out of an apartment.

Boom!

A large blast outside caused frantic tenants to run out of their apartments and run for safety.

"Teagan!" Daughtrey shouted when someone bumped into him and split them up.

"Outside!" Teagan scrambled through the crowd and came back outside. Police and fire trucks surrounded the area and helped to calm the crowd down. Teagan pushed through the crowd to see a car on fire in front of the same spot Sean was shot.

"Stay back!" a policeman yelled.

Teagan started to raise her ID, but Daughtrey caught her arm.

"Not here," Daughtrey said.

"It's them, Daughtrey." Teagan yanked out of his hold.

"We can't make it known, Teagan."

Teagan glanced around the crowd and noticed two men leaning against a car laughing as people cried and needed support.

Teagan whispered in his ear.

"Check your view on the left." Teagan kept her eyes forward.

"You want to take it?"

"Don't make a scene but split up and follow."

"Keep your location on."

"Check in five minutes."

Teagan moved through the crowd and kept an eye on

the police. Then the two men jumped in the car. Teagan motioned for a taxi, hopped in the back, and told him to follow the car in front of them. She texted Daughtrey.

Tegan: We're behind the car.

Daughtrey: Texting Spider and the team.

Teagan: Keep the police away.

The car weaved through traffic and stopped at the light.

"How much further?" the taxi driver questioned.

"Cut the meter. I'll pay you for the rest of the day."

Daughtrey: Spider's heading out now.

The black Audi stopped at a restaurant not far from where the explosion occurred. Teagan looked behind her, and traffic slowed down. She removed money out of her pocket and passed it to him and hopped out of the car.

"Stay close," Teagan said to the taxi driver, strolling to the side of the building out of sight of the men as they talked with another group of men. One looked older with gray hair, a beard, and a protruding belly.

Ring!

"Where are you?" Spider inquired.

"At the restaurant not far from them."

"I see you. Don't move until we get there."

"Daughtrey's on the other side."

"We need to keep a tail on them. The van just pulled up."

"Here I come." Teagan hung up, covered her face with her hand, and climbed in the van driven by Spider. Gregory and Broderick were in the back.

"It's them."

"How do you know?"

"Too easy of a setup."

"I mean it could be a trap for you," Broderick countered. The car came around the corner, and Daughtrey jumped in when he pulled off.

"What did you see?" Teagan ignored Broderick.

"I counted four men. I couldn't add the tracker, but I paid the waiter to put a tap on his clothing," Daughtrey explained.

"Stay over here and wait," Teagan said.

"Look, they're getting back in the car." Spider pointed, starting the van again.

"Stay a car or two back."

Spider nodded and sped up to not get blocked behind a food truck. Teagan's only motivation was to get answers and find out who was behind the entire situation.

"We have a track with visuals of four men from the heat signal," Gregory remarked.

The car arrived at the apartment building. Spider turned to the corner and parked, then everyone jumped out.

"Daughtrey's with me, and Spider and Broderick, you stay back on visuals," Teagan explained.

Spider removed equipment from the car and handed an extra gun to Daughtrey, along with a headpiece and goggles.

"Wait until it gets darker."

"Everyone stay alert. This might not be the end of things."

"We're doing this for Sean." Daughtrey hugged Gregory and Spider.

"You stay close to Daughtrey." Spider clapped Teagan on the back.

"Spider, I'm focused," Teagan answered.

"They went up to what looked like the sixth floor," Gregory answered, motioning at his computer visual.

"I can't wait any longer." Teagan started to walk over to the building.

"Teagan!" Spider shouted, and she ignored him. Daughtrey followed her to catch up.

"She's acting reckless again!" Broderick barked.

"Let her go. We need to get in place," Spider ordered.

CHAPTER 10

*A*fter Spider dropped the equipment in the car, he grabbed his cell and sent a message to Teagan. He was on standby, as was Daughtrey, and the rest of the team went forward with the plan. Jacqueline was safe, but nothing would stop Teagan from capturing each person that set out to hurt her people. All of this became too much for him, and he understood if Teagan wanted to quit after what happened, to focus on her family. Sean's family heard the news of his death and were on their way to the White House to meet with the president. His body was getting flown home. At first, the Italian government wasn't open to providing support, but President Sanders expressed his concerns on how it would look. It would become an international disaster if they were denied any support when the death happened on their soil.

Their private plane was ready to go once they arrived, but Teagan might not leave until she executed the entire cartel. To know Diablo had a wife gave her a disgusting feeling. Sean's life was lost over betrayal. All about revenge to force Teagan out in the open.

"They have five more minutes before they arrive." Broderick peered at the camera footage provided by the goggles Daughtrey wore. Once they breached the barrier of the building and turned the camera footage off, anything traced back would be linked to dummy footage of the same events the prior night.

"If Oskala gets away, we're screwed." Spider stared at the message thread from some of the team at the hospital.

"How did we miss her?" Broderick rubbed his chin in thought.

"Not sure, but she's made it her mission to make Teagan suffer."

"Do you think Teagan was deeply involved with Diablo?" Broderick glanced at Spider.

All of them had done undercover work and had gotten involved in situations where they needed to pretend to fall for someone, but Teagan stayed under for much longer. Broderick thought it could have been one of the reasons she left the Agency—to escape the questions and looks from every time people brought up the case. Spider always could read Teagan, but even he had doubts when it came to her and Diablo.

"I trust her."

"Not the question I asked."

"It's the only answer you'll get from me. What are they doing now?"

Spider stood off to the side of the car and waited to get word if they needed backup. Average citizens went on about their lives, unaware a kidnapping by a terrorist group was only a few feet away.

"They made it inside." Broderick held the camera up to Spider.

"Teagan, can you hear me?" Spider spoke in the earpiece.

A few minutes of silence came over the headset.

"I'm here."

"All clear out here."

"I suggest you tell Spider I need your undivided attention," a soft but commanding voice demanded.

* * *

DAUGHTREY GLANCED from Teagan back to Oskala and her men that stood with guns raised toward their heads. Teagan thought it was too easy at first but knew her commitment to find Jacqueline came at a sacrifice. If this would be her last moment, she was prepared to take out as many of Kingston's men as possible. Oskala motioned for her soldier to grab their guns, and Daughtrey puled the trigger and shot him in the head. Oskala smiled at the death of her men. She wasn't like Diablo who held feelings for anyone working for them. Diablo kept her hidden from the outside world because she was unpredictable and would do anything to get the cartel in the news. Teagan put her hand on Daughtrey's shoulder.

"Oskala, we can talk about this."

Oskala lowered her gun, stepped in Teagan's face, and stared into her eyes.

"I see what Diablo saw in you. Very beautiful."

"You can still live."

"Oh. I've heard about the American negotiations." Oskala winked her left eye at her soldiers, raised her hand, and knocked Daughtrey on the head with the butt of her gun.

"Arghhh!" Daughtrey dropped down to his knees.

"Don't do this, Oskala. Take me instead," Teagan argued.

"Where is my husband?"

"I don't know."

"You know everything, Agent… Red." Oskala paused and tilted her head to the side.

"Diablo is a high-priority witness for the government."

"Where is my husband, Agent Red?" Oskala pointed the gun into Daughtrey's head.

"We don't know!" Teagan shouted.

Boom!

Smoke filled the room from the blast and Spider marched in with more men beside him as Teagan reached out and knocked Oskala's hand away from Daughtrey. Oskala punched Teagan in the face and ran down the hall of the apartment. Teagan choked on the smoke and bent down to help Daughtrey to stand.

"Daughtrey, hold on." Teagan helped him on the couch and took off down the hall.

"Teagan, wait!" Spider shouted.

"Go! I'm fine." Daughtrey ripped his shirt off and tied it around his wound. Teagan jogged through the hallway and down the stairs. She reached Oskala and tried to grab her arm. Oskala turned and smacked her across the face.

"You ruined my life!" Oskala shouted, grabbed Teagan by the hair, and hit her in the stomach. Teagan bent over in pain and coughed, elbowing Oskala in the stomach. Oskala released her hold and ran out of the building.

"Fuck!" Teagan stood and held the side of her stomach. She waved through the smoke, picked up her pace, and left. She saw Oskala run toward a car, jump in, and shoot back at Teagan. To avoid the shot, Teagan ran back to the door and hid until the car pulled off.

"Gregory! Gregory, I need visuals!" Teagan shouted in her headpiece.

A car pulled around back, and Teagan hesitated to get in the car until she saw Spider roll the window down.

"Come on!" Spider yelled, and Teagan took off running toward the car.

"Where's Daughtrey?" Teagan asked, opening a bottle of water.

"Broderick has him."

"Only a car ahead of you," Gregory answered through the headpiece.

"I see them," Spider responded.

"We need to get them alone."

"She's not too far off."

"Where is she staying?" Teagan asked Gregory.

"She's registered at a hotel near the market."

"That was the plan all along," Teagan muttered.

"Take the turn up here and beat them before she gets there," Gregory announced.

"You sure she's going to stop off?" Spider quipped.

"She's a creature of habit."

CHAPTER 11

Oskala stood with a grin on her face and the gun in her hand, motioning for Teagan to place her gun on the floor and step back. Teagan told Spider to stay outside, and she would handle her alone, but the look in her eye reflected that it would get ugly between them.

"You look like his type."

"What do you want, Oskala?"

"Your blood."

"Diablo knew what he wanted."

"You Americans lied and arrested him." Oskala gripped the bottle of tequila, poured some in her glass, and gulped it down, before refilling a second shot.

"My people have the building surrounded."

"Fuck you!" Oskala took a sip. Teagan took that moment to run around the side of the wall, and Oskala sent a shot a few feet away.

"Bitch! Diablo never loved you," Oskala screamed.

Teagan remembered her gun was left on the floor.

"Come out, come out, wherever you are." Oskala laughed.

Teagan removed her vest and holster and threw them to distract her. Oskala came around the corner, and Teagan grabbed her arm with the gun, pushed it upwards, and punched her in the nose.

"Arghh!" Oskala screamed.

Teagan started to wrap her arm around Oskala's neck but was pushed back against the wall.

"Ughhh!" Teagan groaned, and Oskala used her head to pop Teagan in the eye.

"You're going to die today, Teagan Stone," Oskala seethed, bashing her in the head. Teagan stared at the gun in the right corner near her foot.

"Diablo used you; he told me," Teagan taunted.

Oskala's eyes rose in shock.

"Fuck you, bitch!" Oskala launched forward, and Teagan lifted her foot and kicked Oskala back, jumping toward the gun before Oskala could recover, and shot her in the chest.

"Ahhh!" Oskala gasped, blood pouring through her clothes and from her mouth.

Teagan breathed heavily, watching Oskala's slide to the ground, her eyes slowly rolling back.

"Diablo can pick them for sure," Tegan muttered, limped out of the room, and saw Spider and Gregory ready to charge in to help her.

"Call the police; a dead body is left."

* * *

"Soon, we will be landing in New York. Please fasten your seatbelts," the stewardess announced.

"Thank you." Teagan lifted the bottle of water to her lips. She glanced down at her arm wrapped in a bandage.

"I got word that her body was taken to the morgue." Spider ended his call.

"Good, she needed to be put to rest."

"I can't believe we're almost back home," Broderick said, and Teagan stared at him.

"Broderick," Teagan called out.

"Yeah?"

"Did you ever meet Diablo's wife?" Teagan questioned.

Spider glanced at him.

"I had no clue."

"I figured."

The plane landed, and Teagan stood and grabbed her bags, following down the stairs to the black SUVs waiting for the team.

"Take a week off," Teagan told the team.

"What about you?"

"With this, I'll probably take a month off," Teagan joked, watching them load bags in the trunk.

Teagan slid her seatbelt on and laid her head back on the seat.

"Agent Stone, I'm Jason, one of your new details."

"Have you met my family?"

"Yes, ma'am."

"Call me Teagan."

"I'd prefer Agent Stone."

"He preferred to call me boss." Teagan chuckled to herself.

"I'm sorry?"

"Nothing."

The van pulled out of the airport with Spider riding with her, and Gregory tagged along with Daughtrey and Broderick. After dropping Spider off, Jason arrived at Teagan's home and parked. She picked up her bag. For the rest of the night, Teagan checked on her family, ate dinner, and sat in her office after she showered and arranged for Sean to receive an honor for the work he'd done with the Agency. The news reports repeated the video of Sean's body when it arrived home.

Ring!

"Teagan Stone."

"Agent Stone?"

Teagan sat up in her chair in a soft, timid voice.

"This is her."

"Sorry to call you so late. My brother told me to wait."

"Jacqueline?"

"Yes, sorry, this is Jacqueline Anderson."

"You're fine, Jacqueline."

"I just wanted to call and personally thank you again for saving me."

"No need to thank me. I was doing my job." Teagan recalled Jacqueline in the apartment chained to a chair, blindfolded. Nonstop chaos when they busted in the apartment.

Jacqueline sniffed.

"I don't know how I can ever thank you. I thought I would never see my family again."

"Focus on your family."

"I know you lost one of your team members out there."

"Unfortunately, we did, but we all signed up for this work."

"I still have nightmares."

Teagan didn't know how to respond.

"Noah suggested a therapist."

"He's right."

"Maybe. I just have the feeling of anxiety not knowing if this will happen again."

"You can't think like that, Jacqueline."

"I won't hold you any longer but again, thank you, Teagan."

"Get some rest and remember your brother would risk it all for you again."

CHAPTER 12

A week later.

Sean's family held the burial at a family plot, and Teagan decided to bring the kids to pay their respects. Christian held Tatum's hand as she cried in his arms. CJ and Cole wiped their eyes, and Teagan watched the flowers being laid on top of his casket. A few of his family members gave speeches, and the president stood next to the family. A small amount of press was allowed to accompany him. Teagan still held guilt, even though his family gave their gratitude for everything she did trying to save Sean.

"You're ready to go." Christian glanced at the casket being laid in the ground.

"Yeah, we should get the kids home." Teagan and her family headed to their car.

"Teagan."

Teagan paused and motioned for Christian to go ahead to the car when the president approached.

"Mr. President."

"How are you feeling?"

"Feeling ready for work."

"You know it's fine to take some time off."

"Everyone keeps telling me that."

"Oskala's no longer an issue."

"We've interrupted what she was planning with the Kingston Cartel."

"She's been after me for a while."

"Gloria tried to push her agenda."

The president walked alongside Teagan to her car.

"The only thing that matters is that Jacqueline is home safe."

"I saw your press briefing the other day."

"It won't end until they try to find something on the Agency."

"Definitely shown." Teagan stopped in front of her car.

"Thank you again, Teagan. Noah is overjoyed and grateful."

"I did my job, Mr. President," Teagan said.

"A job we know that's not easy."

"You should know." Teagan smirked.

The president reached out for a hug, and Teagan opened the passenger door and climbed in as security walked the president back to the beast.

* * *

LATER THAT DAY, Teagan punched the weight bag in the training room of the Agency, then removed her gloves and walked to the gun range to pick up her weapon. She wiped the sweat off her brow and picked up goggles. Teagan sent off shots and pushed the button to see the target sheet. All the bullets went into the head, Then the door opened, permitting Spider.

"How long have you been hiding down here?"

"Soon as the funeral was over."

"His family wanted to see you at the house."

"It would have been too hard."

"Saw you with the president."

"He just told me about Gloria having an agenda, and I already knew that."

"All politicians have an agenda," Spider replied.

"We have to get better with the people we have on our team."

"How so?"

"Keep a tighter eye on everyone. Oskala was too familiar with our moves."

"What are you saying?"

"Another leak probably, but I can't be sure."

"You sound paranoid."

"I might be paranoid, but with my past, I wouldn't put it past anyone."

"Including me?"

Teagan reloaded her gun and shot at the target.

"Everyone."

Teagan holstered her weapon, removed her goggles, and they stepped on the elevator to head to their office.

Teagan grabbed a change of clothes out of her bag and hopped in the shower.

A few minutes later, she sat at her desk and opened the file on the case. She pulled photos of each person from Oskala, Godfrey, Alex, Arroya, Sean, and Jacqueline. Teagan studied the details and locations of the shop and the distance to travel to the apartment where Alex and Godfrey were found.

Timelines ran over and over in her head, including every step from the moment she got the call of her kidnapping at the store. For a second, she thought of tracking all the calls from the Agency going out.

Ring!

"Hello."

"Are you coming home soon?"

"What time is it?" Teagan raised her wrist up and checked the time.

"Going on eight."

"I didn't know it was that late."

"The kids finished dinner."

"Logging out now. Be home soon."

"See you soon, babe."

"Love you."

"Love you more, Teagan."

Teagan closed the folder and threw it in her bag, turned the light off in her office and strolled to the elevator to leave for the day. A half hour later, Teagan read a book to Tatum, kissed her on the forehead, and tucked her under the comforter. She checked on Cole and CJ, then strolled in her bedroom and saw Christian up with sports on the TV.

"Hey."

"Did you eat?" Christian asked.

"Not hungry." Teagan kicked off her shoes and dropped her bag on the floor.

"You get Tatum to sleep."

"She was waiting for me. I read her a story." Teagan lay on the bed, slid next to him, and wrapped her arm around his waist. Christian rubbed her back.

"Sean's funeral was nice."

"It was."

"What did the president need to talk to you about?"

"He wanted to check in and see how everything is going with me."

Christian pressed a kiss to her forehead.

"CJ has his game coming up."

"Are you going to be able to come?"

"I'll be in the front row."

"I'll make t-shirts." Christian chuckled.

"What's going on with your work?"

"Work is busy, but the family is my priority. I hate to see you going through the loss of your friend."

"I have an appointment with Dr. Falk."

"Is she helping?"

"She's helping me."

"The new detail."

"Are the kids comfortable with them?"

"Yeah, not sure they'll get close like they did with Sean."

Teagan moved out of his arms and sat against the headboard. Christian turned to face her.

"Today was long. Try to sleep, and we can have breakfast after we drop the kids off at school."

"Like a date?" Teagan teased, rubbing the top of his head.

Christian chuckled, leaned forward, and kissed her on the lips.

"It's a date."

CHAPTER 13

D r. Falk talked to her secretary at the desk as Teagan opened the door and pulled the umbrella down. She signed in, and Dr. Falk waved her back. Teagan went into her office and left the coat on the end of the chair.

"Would you like water, tea, or anything?"

"Water is fine."

Teagan crossed her legs and sighed.

Dr. Falk grabbed a bottle of water from the fridge in the corner and handed it over to Teagan. She slipped the lid off and took a sip. Dr. Falk took a seat in her chair, picked up her notepad, and waited for Teagan to talk.

"Whenever you're ready."

"I just buried one of my friends."

"Sorry to hear that."

"Funny, I thought I would be the one to go first in my group."

"How is your team handling everything?"

"Everyone is walking around in a daze."

"How are you and Christian?"

"Good. He's given me space."

Dr. Falk waited for her to continue.

"You think you two need to reconnect without the kids?"

"We are. He wants to take me to a cabin to get away."

"That sounds like something that would be good for the two of you."

"Sean would tell me all the time to go easy on Christian." Teagan chortled.

"Sean thought highly of you two."

"He was like a brother, and my kids are having a hard time with him gone."

"Sean wouldn't want you to fall into a dark place again."

"Do you think I'm a bad person?"

"Do you think you're a bad person?"

"Sometimes. The decisions I've made…"

"And you think Sean's death is the karma for some of those decisions," Dr. Falk inquired.

Teagan clasped her hands together in her lap.

"Deep down, I know I shouldn't feel like that, but if I would have stayed home and let someone else take the lead, maybe Sean would still be alive."

Dr. Falk dropped the pen on top of the pad.

"Teagan, the feelings won't disappear overnight. I want you to start writing in your journal. When someone passes away, it doesn't mean you'll stop the grieving process overnight."

"I used to tell myself I could handle the conversation with my children about grief, but look at me. At my age, I can barely process it myself."

"You're not alone, and you're not invisible from pain."

"But I should be able to protect my people."

Dr. Falk grabbed the box of tissues and passed it over to her.

"Sean did his job."

"I... I... Sean died protecting me." Teagan broke down in tears. Dr. Falk went to sit across from her and grasped her hand in comfort.

"It's okay to cry. Just know you're not betraying anyone when you let the pain release, Teagan."

"Thank you." Teagan cleared her throat.

"How about you go home and spend time with your family. We did enough for today."

Teagan nodded, grabbed her coat and umbrella, and stood to leave.

* * *

HOURS LATER, Teagan watched as the kids played card games in the living room while she cooked baked chicken, rice, and veggies with chocolate cake for dessert.

Knock!

Teagan turned down the stove, walked to the living room, and saw Christian shake hands with Spider, Daughtrey, and the rest of the guys.

"We have company." Tatum jumped up, ran to Spider, and hugged him around his waist.

"What are you doing here?"

"Just left a bar and wanted to check in with you." Spider pinched Tatum on the cheek.

Teagan glanced at Christian.

"We made plenty of food. You guys can pull up a chair," Christian said. Teagan smiled and kissed him on the lips.

"Thank you."

Christian rubbed her back.

"Anything for you."

"So, who's in the lead?" Daughtrey spoke, sitting down next to CJ and picking up some cards.

"Me!" Tatum shouted and plopped down on the floor.

"How did you know we needed this?"

"I know my boss." Spider nudged Teagan's shoulder.

"Tatum, watch Daughtrey. That one can be sneaky," Teagan teased, heading back to the kitchen to finish cooking.

<h1 style="text-align:center">CHAPTER 14</h1>

A month later.

After Tatum helped Christian and Teagan pack up the car, she climbed in the back passenger seat and buckled her seatbelt. CJ had his first basketball game, and the entire family was going to cheer him on, including Teagan, who decided to spend the day with her kids. With everything that happened, her conversations with Dr. Falk helped her to see that she needed more balance and to not take on the guilt lingering in her heart.

"Everybody ready?" Christian looked in the backseat at all the kids. Tatum and Cole wore headphones and watched movies. CJ held his cell phone in his hand and texted his teammates.

"Ready!" everyone answered.

"You good?" Christian watched Teagan zip up her purse and place it on the floor under her feet.

"I'm good, Christian." Teagan leaned over the seat and kissed him.

"Did you get the shirts?" Christian wondered.

"In the trunk... I got everybody's shirt."

"I like this."

"What?" Teagan interlocked their hands.

"You are more laidback, hanging with the family and ditching work."

"Well, I've learned to let the people that work alongside me do their jobs."

Christian lifted her hand and kissed the back of her palm, then backed out of the driveway. He turned the radio up slightly, and Teagan stared out the window. She noticed her new detail behind them at a distance as they drove toward the yellow light and stopped. Once Oskala was eliminated, in the aftermath of Sean's death, Spider interviewed a new person to be her driver and bodyguard for her family. At first, she was in a rush for a change, but she let it happen after a talk with Christian. The kids seemed to be okay with someone new coming into their lives.

Twenty minutes later, they arrived and parked. Christian helped Tatum and Teagan out of the car as CJ grabbed his bag and ran inside.

"Slow down, Cole!" Christian yelled.

"He's your son," Teagan joked, grabbing Tatum's hand and escorting her to the bleachers.

Christian pulled out the shirts and passed one to everyone. Teagan helped Cole and Tatum put their shirts on, then slipped one on and grabbed the phone to start recording. The team was announced, and all the kids ran out in a line and shook hands with the opponents.

"Mommy, I want something to drink." Tatum patted her leg.

"Wait until they announce your brother, then Daddy will grab some snacks."

Teagan kissed her forehead, and Tatum clapped her hands in excitement.

The doors of the school opened again, and everyone

clapped while Teagan looked on in shock that Spider, Daughtrey, Gregory, and Broderick came to the game in shirts with CJ's number on the front. All the men hyped up the team and came around to the section where Teagan and Christian were sitting.

"What are you guys doing here?" Teagan leaned in to hug them.

"Just in the neighborhood and thought we'd come check out a game," Daughtrey joked, sitting next to Cole.

Gregory and Broderick sat in front of the first row of bleachers, with Spider on the opposite end of Teagan.

"You didn't have to do this."

"All your family and all Sean talked about was this game."

"He loved the kids."

"Relax and watch Daughtrey lose a hundred bucks," Spider teased, winking his left eye at Teagan.

"He did not bet on my child?"

"This is Daughtrey we're talking about."

Teagan shook her head, screaming when they announced CJ's name. This was the only place Teagan wanted to be, and she was glad to have friends and family around to keep her mind from going to that dark palace.

* * *

MONDAY AFTER THE WEEKEND.

Teagan stepped off the elevator and smiled at the security guard and waved at a few other familiar faces while walking down to the conference room for her monthly meeting with the secretary of defense. Today, her hair had been blown out and was down, she wore light makeup, and she looked refreshed and ready for the business at hand. After she scanned her badge and stepped in, she walked to the table that held a classified brief on top. Only the top security clearance was allowed in this meeting, and Teagan wasn't sure if she would be back in after everything that happened.

The secretary of defense spoke on the latest cases that are on high alert for the US. Teagan sat stoic as he spoke on what each agency would handle after the crisis with Jacqueline was over, and she was home safe.

"Agent Stone, you and your team will take on surveillance for now."

"Yes, sir."

"Nothing out of the ordinary, but I want your people to monitor conversations we've recorded."

"Can I ask what the case is about, sir?"

"At this moment, we need to keep it on a need-to-know basis."

"Of course, Mr. Secretary."

Teagan took notes and waited for him to release everyone.

"Mrs. Stone!" He stopped her before she could leave.

"Yes."

"I know it's a difficult time for you right now."

"I'm fine."

"Then you know what's about to happen in London?"

"Not familiar." He scanned the room and waited for the last person to walk out of the room.

"I have reason to believe someone higher up in the London government is planning an attack."

"Has this been confirmed?"

"You're the first person I'm telling."

"My job is to know when something is going to cause an interruption to our priorities."

"Are you ready for a new case? Like mentally prepared?"

"What are you saying?"

"Dr. Falk is a great listener."

Teagan stumbled back in surprise.

"Don't worry, your conversations are strictly confidential."

"How… How did you know?"

"The notepad you're writing on; I have the same one with her logo."

Teagan looked down at her pen and pad.

"My team is ready for anything," Teagan replied.

"Agent Red, I'll be in touch." He held a hand out, and Teagan reached her palm over before watching him leave. She glanced down at her notepad, ripped off the top part, dropped the pad in the trashcan, and headed back to her office.

* * *

I HOPE you enjoyed Teagan's story so far. Please check out **"Agent Red (Revenge) Teagan Stone Book 7"** sneak peek with a host of characters intertwined. Also, if you love mystery, suspense and thriller, check out **"Mirror of Lies Book 1" here** https://books2read.com/u/mgjEPx or another thriller/crime fiction **"Mirror of Lust Book 2" here** https://books2read.com/u/mVRpz2

Check out free short here *"The Firm"* https://payhip.com/b/py7S

Grab Boxset **"Agent Red 1-3"** here https://payhip.com/b/1KcxY

When enemies decide to plot together and bring down a friendly ally, it takes more than the team to get things under control. Will it come at a cost bigger than her job? Her family can only hope she comes home night after night, but things turn upside down when she's put in a terrible situation beyond her control.

READING ORDER OF SERIES

1. Agent Red-Fatal Memory Book 1
https://books2read.com/u/4j2PYX
2. Agent Red-Fatal Target Book 2
https://books2read.com/u/bWP8Jq
3. Agent Red-Fatal Crime Book 3
https://books2read.com/u/mZadZJ
4. Agent Red-Fatal Justice Book 4
https://books2read.com/u/mq07wd
5. Agent Red-Fatal Enemy Book 5
https://books2read.com/u/bxe01q
6. Agent Red-Fatal Death Book 6
https://books2read.com/u/bQy5qP
7.Agent Red-Fatal Revenge Book 7

Mirror of Lies Book 1
   https://books2read.com/u/mgjEPx
   Mirror of Lust Book 2
   https://books2read.com/u/mVRpz2
   Mirror of Danger Book 3
   Mirror of Murder Book 4

WHAT'S NEXT?

Want to know what happens next? Follow me at the links below to catch the next release.

Thank you so much for reading, and if you enjoyed the crazy ride and decide to leave a review, we'd truly appreciate the support. Reviews are the lifeblood of the publishing world. They're read, appreciated, and needed. Please consider taking the time to leave a few words on Goodreads or BookBub.

Sign up for updates and sneak peeks at the sites below:
www.authoravasking.com

ACKNOWLEDGMENTS

I want to thank my team, who helps me behind the scenes, from my editors to my test readers and graphic designers, and the list goes on. I truly appreciate each of you for keeping me on my toes.

ABOUT THE AUTHOR

Ava S. King writes mystery, psychological crime thrillers, international espionage thrillers, political and action/adventure novels. Her debut novel, Agent Red Fatal Memory became a huge hit with100 BestSellers, Top Indie Favorite. 100 Debut release on all digital platforms. Born and raised in TN, filmmaker and lover of all things mystery and suspense. In addition to writing, Ava loves bringing her novels to life on the bigscreen starting with Agent Red series.

ABOUT 304 PUBLISHING COMPANY

We showcase authors writing African American, interracial, women's fiction, urban romance, erotica, and contemporary romance novels, along with thrillers, suspense novels, poetry collections, and beauty & style books.www.304publishing.com

www.ingramcontent.com/pod-product-compliance
Lightning Source LLC
Chambersburg PA
CBHW011202190726
48286CB00009B/2888